Bend Toward the Sun

Bend Toward the Sun

JEN DEVON

ST. MARTIN'S
GRIFFIN

NEW YORK

First published in the United States by St. Martin's Griffin, an imprint of St. Martin's Publishing Group

BEND TOWARD THE SUN. Copyright © 2022 by Jen Devon. All rights reserved. Printed in the United States of America. For information, address St. Martin's Publishing Group, 120 Broadway, New York, NY 10271.

www.stmartins.com

Designed by Kelly S. Too

Library of Congress Cataloging-in-Publication Data

Names: Devon, Jen, 1978– author.
Title: Bend toward the sun / Jen Devon.
Description: First edition. | New York : St. Martin's Griffin, 2022.
Identifiers: LCCN 2022006001 | ISBN 9781250822000 (trade paperback) | ISBN 9781250822017 (ebook)
Subjects: LCGFT: Romance fiction. | Novels.
Classification: LCC PS3604.E8873 B46 2022 | DDC 813/.6—dc23/eng/20220217
LC record available at https://lccn.loc.gov/2022006001

Our books may be purchased in bulk for promotional, educational, or business use. Please contact your local bookseller or the Macmillan Corporate and Premium Sales Department at 1-800-221-7945, extension 5442, or by email at MacmillanSpecialMarkets@macmillan.com.

First Edition: 2022

10 9 8 7 6 5 4 3 2 1

For Keith. You're my favorite.

PART ONE

CHAPTER ONE

Rowan

Rowan McKinnon crouched in an abandoned greenhouse in the rural Pennsylvania darkness, trying not to pee her pants. She'd have taken it a bit easier on the Cabernet tonight if she'd known the party at the old vineyard would include a game of hide-and-seek.

The greenhouse was a good hiding place for a botanist. Rowan was wildly curious to see what grew there in the light of day. The clouded glass ceiling was tall and cathedral-shaped, allowing only enough silvery moonlight through to see the place was a mess. Wooden floorboards were warped by moisture and fuzzy with moss. Beneath vented roof panels, little islands of plants overflowed pots to ramble across a maze of tables and benches. Life had flourished and thrived there, despite years of apparent neglect.

Rowan felt a pang of kinship.

In the darkness outside, someone's scream dissolved into laughter, the sound followed by whoops of triumphant men's voices. The hairs on the back of Rowan's neck involuntarily rose.

"Just a game," she murmured, shifting her weight from foot to foot.

Four weeks ago, she'd packed up her two suitcases of

belongings and left Cornell to head back to Philadelphia. Philly wasn't home—nowhere was, really—but Temperance and Frankie were still there. The three of them had been best friends since undergrad, and Rowan needed a quiet place to revise her research manuscript. Only days after she'd defended her dissertation, her department chair had called to report "significant complications" about her data sets. Suddenly, her world of stable, deliberate plans became a world of roadblocks and uncertainties. She couldn't publish until she did major recalculations and rewrites, and she couldn't apply for worthwhile postdoctoral fellowships until she published.

Couldn't recognize herself without that academic lens.

Couldn't manage to peel herself off Temperance's couch.

Frankie had visited early in the week, unable to entice Rowan out of her funk even with the promise of Robustelli's cheesesteaks and famous truffle Parmesan fries. Rowan had instead subsisted exclusively on caramel popcorn and cherry soda for days, watching and rewatching David Attenborough's *The Private Life of Plants* and repotting her small collection of succulents in Temperance's little kitchen.

Rowan wondered if Temperance would have still dragged her along tonight if she'd have pantomimed self-care by conspicuously eating a banana or an apple a time or two. Maybe Temperance would have left her alone if she'd managed to change out of her pajamas. At least once.

Tonight's revelry was a housewarming party to celebrate the Brady family's new ownership of the property. Temperance was a de facto member of the Brady family—her older sister, Maren, was married to one of the Brady sons. Rowan grudgingly found the Bradys charming, but they had big-family camaraderie, the kind of overt, playful loudness that came from a lifetime of knowing exactly who your people were. It was a stark, slap-in-the-face contrast to her own lonely childhood, and being there in the midst of it, she felt as conspicuous as a toad on a birthday cake. *"Like recognizes like,"* her mother always used to say. Even as a child Rowan had been able to infer that "like" also recognized *other*.

So, she'd sipped wine—a lot of it—around the bonfire, introverting like a card-carrying professional, until she was unceremoniously opted in to the hide-and-seek game by a determined Temperance and Frankie. "Team Tag" the Bradys called it, a decades-old tradition at their family gatherings. A handsome older man in a barbecue apron emblazoned with WELL SEASONED—presumably the Brady patriarch, William—had stood on a picnic table to belt out the game's rules for the newcomers. Teams were the Brady family versus non-Bradys. Timed rounds, whoever captures the most members of the other team in thirty minutes wins. Everyone got a little pocket flashlight, for safety. They were all branded with BRADY BROTHERS CONTRACTING in typeface straight from the 1980s. Cute.

The only family traditions Rowan had were trips to Kmart with Grandma Edie for new shoes before each new school year, and hot cocoa from cheap powdered packets on Christmas Eve. Imagine having an entire *game* as a tradition. With branded swag.

When Rowan had arrived, her eyes had been drawn to the Victorian-style greenhouse on the rise at the top of the property. The glass panes had shone like amethysts in the sunset. But now that she was inside it, the big building had lost its whimsy. The white metal frame instead seemed to hunch over her like a massive skeletal rib cage.

Even before academic calamity had her spiraling into existential self-doubt, Rowan had always been an anxious, awkward sort. For kids and well-adjusted adults, this game was probably pure, primal adrenaline-tripping. A thrill of imminent danger, with no real-world consequences. But Rowan had no childhood frame of reference to compare to, no baseline to determine whether her sprinting pulse and sweaty neck were typical, or overreactions.

She was hurtling toward thirty and had never played hide-and-seek.

As she'd raced across a wide lawn and up the hill after the starting whistle blew, a latecomer's car headlights briefly illuminated her as it pulled up the gravel drive. Aside from that, there'd been no sign she'd been seen or followed.

Until now.

A shadow passed across the glass at the front of the greenhouse.

"Just a game," she reminded herself again. Sweat was slippery behind her knees. Her rapid breathing was strangely muffled by the dense greenery and heavy air. Late summer humidity made copper curls pull free from her braid, coiling outward in serpentine mayhem around her face. She blew the strands back and peeked over the edge of the potting cabinet she'd chosen for cover. Silence.

Shoes skidded on the gravel outside the greenhouse door. Rowan gasped, clumsily brandishing the little flashlight like a weapon.

A wide-shouldered, undeniably male form filled the doorway, backlit by the weak porch lamp outside. He made a little "gah" sound as her light hit him in the eyes. In the narrow beam, Rowan took rapid inventory of him: body lanky, very tall. Golden hair, winging from the sides of a frayed ball cap. Thin, angular face, new beard—and not the well-managed, trendy kind. It was the scruff of a man who couldn't be bothered to shave, let alone give any shits about beard combs and balms.

Being discovered so quickly wouldn't have been a problem, really. She'd simply go drink more wine around the fire while everyone else played out the game.

The *problem* was—this rangy, disheveled man wasn't someone she recognized from the party. By his height alone, Rowan certainly would have remembered him.

She snapped the flashlight off and tucked it into the pocket of her cutoffs. She pivoted, leaping over a knee-high bench.

"Hey!" the man said. Footfalls thudded on creaky floorboards as he gave chase.

Rowan heard a smack and answering groan as he slammed into one of the heavy tables. Then, a burst of filthy, breathless words. The baritone rasp of his voice drew goose bumps across her skin like a needle pulling thread.

Jumping a few more short benches, Rowan shoved several stacks of plastic nursery pots off a table, sending them tumbling in the direction opposite from the one she headed in. While the pots clattered to the ground, she froze, using the commotion for cover. She opened her mouth wide to catch her breath. Her tongue felt as dry as old newspaper.

Again, she heard the unmistakable crack of a shin or ankle bone meeting wood. A groan, and "Mother*fucker.*" Then he went as quiet as her.

A solitary cricket whirred once, twice, testing the silence. Outside, another bubbly scream split the night, followed by peals of familiar, obnoxious laughter. Frankie must have gotten caught. It annoyed Rowan that she couldn't force her brain to find that same uncomplicated joy in the experience.

Could she get around the guy and out the front door? Possibly, if she could pinpoint where he was and get him moving in the wrong direction before she made her break. But the tables and benches weren't arranged in any pattern. It had been sheer luck she hadn't yet tripped ass over ankles and busted out a tooth.

From where she squatted, the wide windows along the back wall of the greenhouse were far closer than the front door. One of them was cracked open.

She could get there.

A rumbly sigh came from an indeterminate place in the shadows. "I think you're out of bounds, this far away from base." His voice was smoother now that it wasn't grinding out obscenities. It had a cultured cadence to it that opposed his rumpled appearance.

Was he *teasing* her?

Rowan caught her lips between her teeth and fought the impulse to retort. He'd homed in on the only thing that might make her give away her position—and her advantage: an accusation that she wasn't following the rules.

At least she knew now he was part of the game, and not some vagrant from Linden, the closest town over on the way back to Philly. Still, it seemed strange she hadn't seen him until now. Maybe he'd been the latecomer in the car. That would explain why he didn't have a flashlight.

Rowan's knees and ankles burned from crouching, and *god*, her bladder.

Outside, two male voices shouted to each other from different directions, coordinating with militaristic urgency. Moments later, another high-pitched scream floated up the hill before dissolving into giggles. Her teammates were dropping like flies.

A plastic pot rolled across the floor in the darkness. Her pursuer was on the move, but heading toward the wrong side of the greenhouse, by the sound of it. Rowan seized the opportunity, shooting to her feet to make for the back wall.

The guy went down again as he tried to swivel and pursue. This time, his growling groan sounded muffled, like his mouth was pressed against the ground. She almost felt sorry for him, but her haywire sense of self-preservation wouldn't let her stop to check on him.

Rowan wanted to shout with relief as her hand closed on the lever-like handle of the partially open window at the back of the greenhouse. She grasped the latch in both hands and shoved, hard.

Nothing.

No movement. It was frozen into a foot-wide opening by rust and time.

Shit.

As circulation returned, her legs felt like they were full of buzzing bees. The eruption of sensation nearly buckled her knees. She blurted an agonized, frantic laugh.

"No way you're getting through that," the guy called. He grunted, pushing to his feet.

Rusty joints screamed like a banshee and the pane gave. She pushed it up and outward, as wide as it would go, then dipped her head through. Way too far down to go headfirst.

Rowan hooked each of her legs through the bottom lip of the window, squeezing her backside through with a shimmy of her hips. For a mortifying moment, she imagined becoming stuck, wedged there between the glass, squished out like a specimen on a microscope slide.

"Told you."

His smug tone pissed her off. Squeezing her butt tight, she wiggled centimeters farther out the window. She'd make it. There were still too many tables between them for him to reach her before she was fully through. A petty surge of triumph buoyed her.

But then, everything changed. When Rowan looked back again, he was retreating, fading quickly away in the darkness.

He headed for the door.

Oh, god. He was going to intercept her outside.

"Shit, shit, *shit,*" Rowan wheezed. She'd wedged too far into the window to pull herself back inside, and her feet hadn't hit the ground yet, so she had no leverage. She dangled there, inert, limp as a flag on a windless day.

It was a miracle her shorts hadn't ripped yet. With a desperate final squeeze of her ass, she made it the rest of the way through the window, hitting the ground below with a molar-clacking impact.

"Just a game," she panted.

The guy was already around the side of the greenhouse, and the moon seemed to shine a spotlight on her. Adrenaline pumped wildfire into her bloodstream. But it didn't matter. His legs were longer, and he had a head start.

In a few long strides, his arms snapped around her torso like a living straitjacket. "You're caught. You're done," he said, his breath igniting a hot trail from her earlobe to her collarbone.

Cinnamon gum.

The primitive part of her brain did a strange double-duty analysis, acknowledging the alarm of being caught, while simultaneously detecting that her captor smelled *delicious.* Somehow like marshmallows, undercut with sharp, peppery juniper and clean sweat. That weird juxtaposition of sensory delight with the compounded anxiety from the entire evening made her light-headed.

More screams in the distance, more laughter, more hoots of victory from male voices. Really, had the rest of her team hidden behind bushes and tree trunks?

Rowan jerked against his grip.

"Easy," the guy said, letting his arms fall away. At the same time, she twisted to face him to push free, and the momentum made her bounce her nose sharply against his breastbone like a choreographed slapstick gag.

Phantom stars instantly bloomed behind her eyes, a firework of pain. Tears welled, her scalp prickled. The stranger reached out and slid his hands down the backs of her arms, clutching lightly to keep her steady.

Rowan moaned into her cupped hands.

"Damn it, sorry. Let me see." He removed his ball cap, and a boyish swoop of hair fell over his forehead. He tossed the locks back with an upward jerk of his chin, then reseated the cap bill-backward on his head. Gently, he cuffed her wrists and pulled her hands away from her nose.

"Bleeding?" she mumbled.

"Ah, you *can* speak." He tucked a knuckle under her chin to tilt her face to the moonlight, bringing his face close to hers.

Rowan glared. It was her first real look at him in the glow of the moon. His height disoriented her—she wasn't used to having to look up to meet someone's eyes. His clothes were too big for his lean frame. Hollows bracketed his mouth beneath too-sharp cheekbones. The edges of gleaming white teeth showed beneath a vaguely snarly top lip as he struggled to catch his breath.

There was an intangible vulnerability about him that tempered her combativeness. Something about his posture, or the way his concerned frown made his eyebrows dip down at the outer edges. The backward ball cap, or the spicy scent of his gum.

One of his hands maintained a warm, proprietary grip on her arm, his thumb absently passing up and down her bicep. His other hand cupped her opposite elbow. Awareness stirred inside her—an explicit human-to-human recognition of warm, healthy skin against her own. Somehow, this entire bizarre situation was beginning to turn her on, muddling her instinct to run.

Of *course* her libido would make this even weirder.

"I look like a goblin shark now, don't I?" she said. Her voice sounded nasally to her own ears, but the tingling pain had already faded, urged on its way by the long-fingered hands steadying her. Soothing her.

"Ah—I'm not sure if I should take you straight to an emergency room or a reconstructive surgeon."

His expression was placid on the surface, but something in his eyes churned like a rip current. As he studied her face, Rowan caught a glimpse of his tongue, nudging against the tip of a perfect incisor.

"Ha, ha," she deadpanned.

While evading him in the dark greenhouse, her rampaging imagination had painted him as a faceless wraith. A thing devoid of personhood. But now that she was close enough to him that she *smelled* his body heat and felt the gusts of his breath against her mouth, it was impossible to ignore his very appealing humanity.

With a lover's familiarity, he tucked a loose curl behind her ear. The pads of his fingertips brushed along the sensitive curve of the lobe. "You good now?" he said. His eyes dipped to her lips. It sent a sucker punch of desire straight to her belly.

She didn't know his name.

The narrow space between them changed and charged, like the air pressure plunge before a major storm. They breathed each other, inhaling what the other exhaled. The greedy ache in her belly unwound and spread lower until it found a home between her hip bones. Rowan tipped her head back and narrowed her eyes in silent challenge, daring him to make a move.

Did people hook up at housewarming parties?

She didn't *need* to know his name for that.

A few flyaway filaments of her hair floated upward, caressing his face. He dipped his head subtly to the side, questioning, calculating. A modest forward nudge, a deeper downward exhale, and his mouth would be on hers. Curiosity and panic and recklessness expanded in her chest like an intoxicant-filled balloon.